PAUL BUNYAN'S SWEETHEART

By Marybeth Lorbiecki & Illustrated by Renée Graef

To Aunt Mary (Mary Williams),
a real Lucette, with a heart as big as the north woods.

Marybeth

For Tim, my mother, Rhonda, and Mary.

Renée

Sleeping Bear Press™

310 North Main Street, Suite 300
Chelsea, MI 48118
www.sleepingbearpress.com

THOMSON
∗
GALE™

© 2007 Thomson Gale, a part of the Thomson Corporation.

Thomson, Star Logo and Sleeping Bear Press are trademarks
and Gale is a registered trademark used herein under license.

Printed and bound in the United States.

First Edition

10 9 8 7 6 5 4 3 2 1

Library of Congress Cataloging-in-Publication Data

Lorbiecki, Marybeth.
Paul Bunyan's sweetheart / written by Marybeth Lorbiecki ; illustrated by Renée Graef.
p. cm.
Summary: When legendary logger Paul Bunyan falls in love with Lucette Diana Kensack, he will
do whatever it takes to win her heart, including trying to restore the Minnesota environment
to its previous condition as part of Lucette's "love test."
ISBN 13: 978-1-58536-289-9
1. Bunyan, Paul (Legendary character)—Juvenile fiction. [1. Bunyan, Paul (Legendary character)—
Fiction. 2. Love—Fiction. 3. Nature—Effect of human beings on—Fiction. 4. Environmental
degradation—Fiction. 5. Minnesota—History—To 1858—Fiction. 6. Tall tales.] I. Graef, Renée, ill.
II. Title.
PZ7.L8766Pau 2007
[E]—dc22
2006026583

FOREWORD

Remember Paul Bunyan—that giant lumberjack who scattered towering pines like toothpicks, using some to clean his teeth? He and his ox, Babe the Blue, tramped from Maine to Oregon, leaving gaping footprints that filled up with rainwater to make lakes. They helped turn the trees of North America into lumber for houses and businesses.

But a man as big as Paul gets a little lonely.

That was until he wandered over to Hackensack, Minnesota where he met Lucette Diana Kensack.

Lucette's mother was an Ojibwe maiden and her father was a French-English pioneer. The sad thing was, an illness called smallpox came through. It wiped out Miss Kensack's family. Thankfully a big mama bear took pity on that eight-year-old and let her join her cubs.

It may have been the pox, or it may have been the berries, but Lucette started growing and growing and growing. She grew so tall she couldn't fit into that bear's cave or any ordinary cabin. So when she wandered into Hackensack, the people slung a roof between two fire towers and built her some rooms.

Paul had heard stories about this woman, but he didn't believe them. They sounded like pretty tall tales!

Lucette Diana Kensack was one joyous, ample gal, with a cow to match. Her cow, Nel, had once been hit by lightning, sparking and sputtering and inflating like a hot air balloon till she was big as a cabin.

With all Nel's milk, Lucette would churn up a thick creamy river. Her neighbors scooped up whatever butter they needed. How do you think those midwestern states came to be known as the dairy states?

And what a quilter Lucette was! Her neighbors were always asking her to make one for them, forty acres square, with seeds sewed in rowed stitches—corn and squash, pumpkin and beans, wheat and barley and oats. She'd shake those quilts out and lay them on the ground. Within days those folks had farm fields growing up, pretty as you please.

When summer heat hung down like boiling syrup, the townsfolk would ask Lucette to shake out her rugs. If she'd do it gentle like, her breezes would cool the sweat off their bodies so quick they'd have to hold on to their clothes to keep them on.

But sometimes Lucette would get so enthusiastic she'd send tornadoes swirling to Texas. This happened so often during spring and fall cleaning spells that folks came to naming the southern path of those winds Tornado Alley!

One spring cleaning day, Lucette sent those winds Paul Bunyan's way. Suddenly he smelled something so delectable blowing toward him, he raced like a forest fire to Hackensack. Then he stopped in his tracks.

Lucette Diana Kensack was a sight to behold. Her hair was as dark and glossy as a black bear's fur, and her eyes were the color of a piney hill on a misty morning. She was tossing big globs of what looked like hot lava into a bucket with the last of the winter snow.

Paul snatched up a blob
and popped it in his mouth.

"Robber!" she shouted and
bopped him on the head.

"That's my rock candy!" Lucette complained. "I boiled up maple sap and swirled in my strawberry, blueberry, and thimbleberry jams." (People nowadays call Lucette's rock candy Lake Superior agates.)

Paul's heart pounded like an ax on a tree, cutting him apart. He managed to spit out with a grin, "Why, Miss Lucette, your candy's as sweet as you, and I couldn't resist."

She eyed him, but didn't bop him again.

"I'm Paul Bunyan and people say I'm the biggest, strongest, and most handsome man around. Don't you think we'd make a might perfect couple?" he crooned, lovesick.

Miss Lucette burst forth with a laugh livelier than fiddle music. "What makes you think I need someone big and strong and handsome? Don't I look like I've been taking care of myself just fine?"

All of a sudden, Paul felt as cornered as a cougar in a cave. If he said no, he'd insult her. If he said yes, he'd admit she didn't need him. "Any woman could use a man who'll put all his strength and cleverness into loving her good and proper, don't you think?"

"Are you willing to prove it in a love test?" she asked, dimpling. "I've got three tasks."

It was Paul's turn to laugh, a big bellowy bark that blew the shutters off her cabin windows and the hair off her dog, Pickles. "You betcha! Give me my tasks!" he declared.

She smiled. "Okay. Summer's coming. Task number one: Can you make this land spread out feathery and cool and dappled like a princess's fairyland?"

Paul's eyes widened big as windows. "I'll get right to work on it," he said, and he hightailed it out of there, thinking all the way.

When he got back to the lumber camp, he sat down with his buddies, Joe Birch and Tom Mile. They'd never seen him so smitten!

So Paul and his friends caught all the Canada geese they could and plucked them clean. He layered the goose feathers atop nets spread overhead from poles. Proud of himself, Paul went to fetch Lucette.

But just as she got there, a wind whistled through, taking the goose down with it. A passel of angry naked geese came pecking at Paul's feet.

Lucette just grinned. "Maybe you'd like to try task number two?"

"Can you make the lake sparkle like a bowl full of diamonds?"

That sounded easier to Paul, so off he went.

The lake was murky from the dirt washed into it after the logging. Paul couldn't figure how to clean it up, so he put his shaving mirror on top of corks to float on the lake. That sure made it sparkly!

Paul went to find his love.

But just as Lucette walked up, a flock of ducks zoomed in and shattered that mirror to pieces! A passel of angry ducks came quacking at Paul's head.

Lucette sighed and shook her head. "How about trying the last task?"

Paul nodded grimly. He'd never failed at anything, and now he'd done it twice.

"Can you make the air smell as fine as French perfume?"

"You bet!" Paul shouted.

So Paul went to ask his friend Pierre Le Coeur, the voyageur, to bring him boxes and boxes of French perfume.

Paul had to wait weeks for those little bottles to arrive. He couldn't eat, he couldn't sleep, he just mooned away to darn near nothin'. Even his blue ox started turning purple 'cause Paul was so blue and moody.

Finally Pierre delivered the perfume. Paul and his friends snuck out to a spot they'd logged not far from Lucette's cabin. The sun blistered down as they uncorked bottle after bottle and poured it in a vat. Then Paul picked up his fireplace bellows and started to fan that perfume.

In no time at all, Lucette came rushing out of her cabin, her apron held to her nose, screeching, "What in tarnation is that smell?" Even Nel was coughing.

Paul's heart sank. That perfume didn't smell so good after sitting in the sun. Now he'd never have lovely Lucette.

But funny thing was, Lucette just started to laugh and laugh, till all the flowers and vegetables were dancing from her breath. "You tried your best, and that's all a gal can ask. Now, let me show you the easiest answers to my love tests."

"Have you ever looked around the woods after you're through? They're a mess! I can't go marrying a man who expects me or someone else to clean up after him!"

Paul felt like a giant pine had just fallen on him. "What are you saying?"

"I'm saying I need me some shade and fine-smelling woods and a sparkling lake for a good swim. So if you want to show me you love me, Paul, start planting trees where you've cut them. And start saving trees around lakes and streams. You need to become an all-around man of the woods—a forester!"

Paul hadn't heard that word before but he liked it. It sounded strong and tall, like him. Lucette showed him how to use one of her sewing needles to prick the soil and insert a little seedling, just like a bead on a moccasin. But for this kind of woodland sewing, she made sure he did not sew in rows!

So Paul and his lumberjack buddies spent the rest of the summer planting all different kinds of trees, especially pines, and he won the heart of Lucette Diana Kensack.

They were married the next year, on June 9, 1838, by Judge Edward Little, with his lumber-buddies-turned-foresters Joe and Tom as witnesses.

From then on, Paul Bunyan never forgot to clean up after himself and leave the land as healthy as he found it.

And Lucette happily spent her days near Hackensack, where she could stroll through forest fairylands, swim in sparkling lakes, and smell those piney fresh woods.